Rocking Horse Christmas

BY MARY POPE OSBORNE ❧ PAINTINGS BY NED BITTINGER

SCHOLASTIC INC.

New York Toronto London Auckland Sydney
Mexico City New Delhi Hong Kong Buenos Aires

The boy found the rocking horse
under the tree.
He pushed it softly
and made it rock.
"I'll call you Shadow," he said.
Then he climbed on Shadow's back,
and they took off.

They rocked to the West—
and lassoed an outlaw.

They rocked to the East—
and jousted with knights.
They rocked all Christmas day.

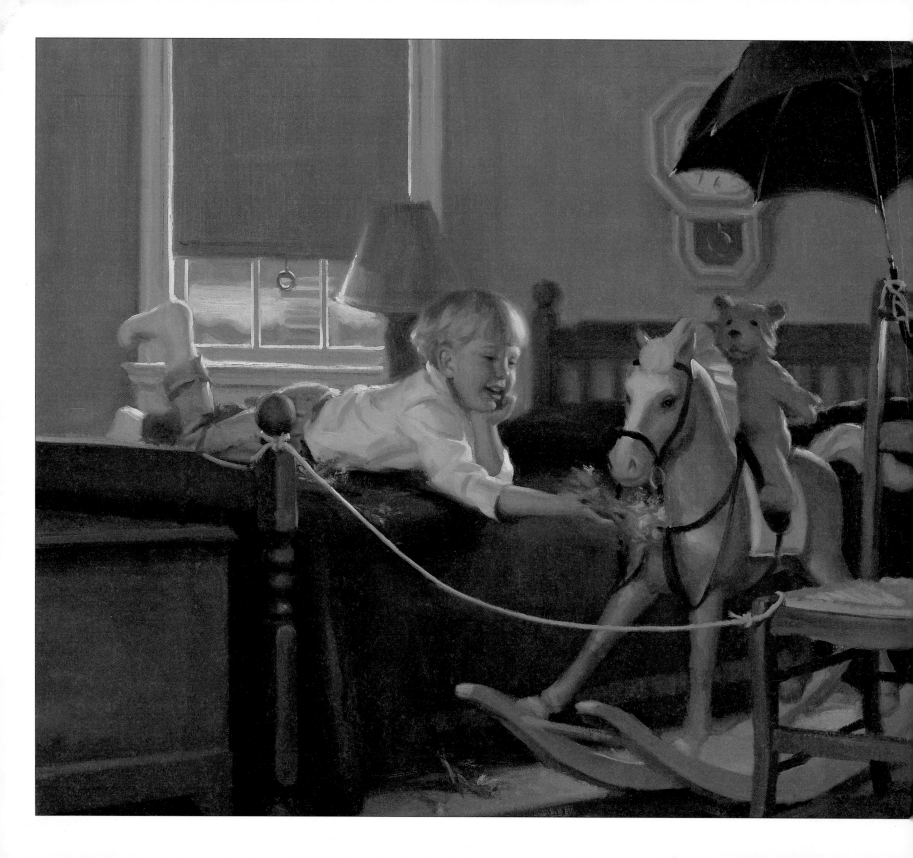

Then the boy carried Shadow
up to his room.
He made a little stall
beside his bed
and fed Shadow some hay.

Shadow and the boy
rocked together day after day.

They went on a safari
on an African plain.

They raced Seattle Slew
in the Kentucky Derby.

They rode to the land of dinosaurs
and fought a Tyrannosaurus rex.

Every night, before sleep,
the boy touched Shadow's mane.
"Ride you tomorrow," he'd whisper.

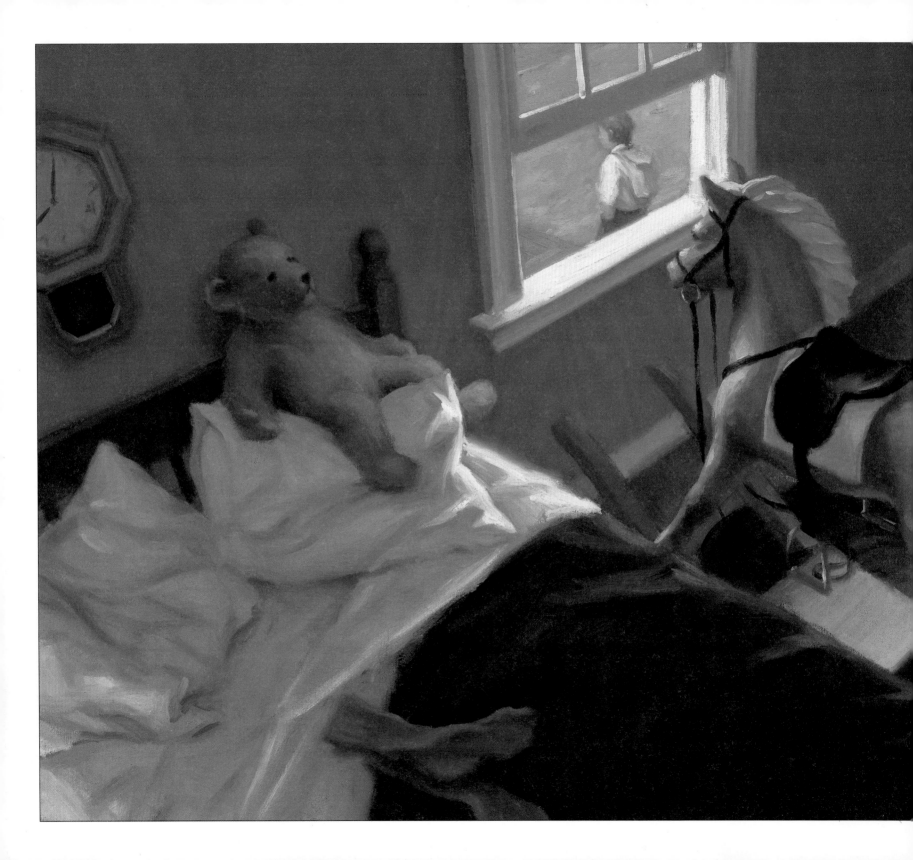

But as the boy got older,
he didn't ride Shadow as much.
And then, days and weeks
and months went by
when he didn't ride Shadow at all.

Hour after hour,
the rocking horse stood still,
waiting to rock while
the clock ticked away.
"I know how you feel," said the old bear
who now stared sadly into space.

One day, someone
picked Shadow up
and carried him to the attic.

There he grew dusty and frail.
A spider strung a web between his ears.
"You must have been a great horse once,"
she said.

Year after year,
the rocking horse stared out the window,
looking for his boy.

Sometimes he saw a boy
playing catch in the yard
or riding a bike down the street.
But *this* boy was much taller
than *his* boy.

Once he saw a young man
who looked a bit like his boy
load a car and drive away.

Another time he saw a man visit
with a woman and a baby.

Brown leaves fell,
and green leaves returned.
But Shadow's boy never came back.

Then one year,
on Christmas Eve,
a blizzard struck.
Glass broke,
and the winds knocked Shadow over.
Soon he was covered
with a blanket of snow,
and his spirit began to fade.

Suddenly the hatch door opened,
and light streamed in.
Then Shadow heard something
he hadn't heard in a long time—
a boy's voice.
"Look, Dad," the boy said.
"The storm broke the window."

"Watch out for glass," a man said.
He knelt down. "Hey, look at this."
"What is it, Dad?"
The man wiped the snow
from Shadow's head.
Shadow looked into the man's eyes
and knew at once who he was.
"He's my oldest friend in the world,"
the man said.

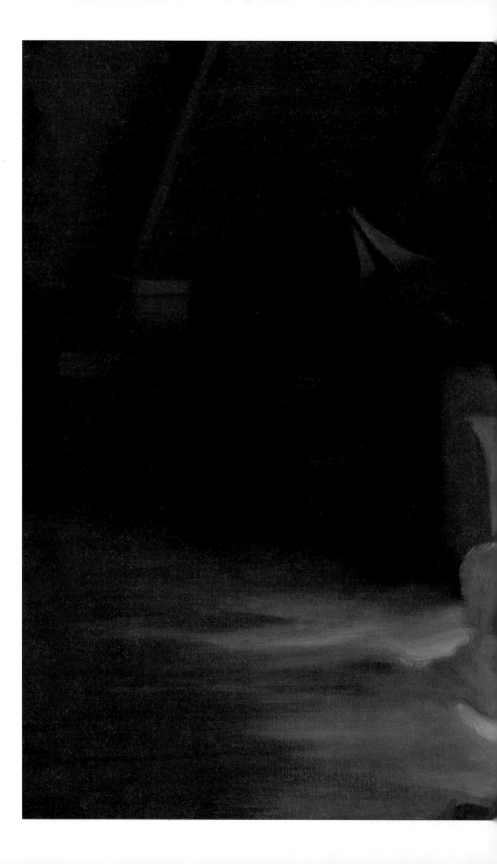

The man carried the
rocking horse downstairs.
They made a little stall
in the dining room
and fed him some hay.
"What's his name, Dad?" the boy asked.
"Shadow," the man said.
"Hi, Shadow," the boy whispered.
Then he climbed on Shadow's back.
"Giddyap," he said.
At first Shadow was creaky.
But then his heart took a leap…

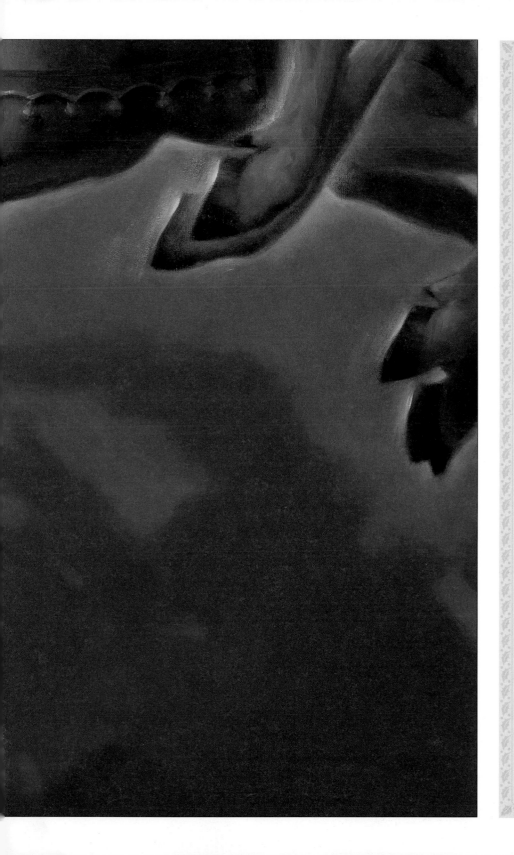

...and he and the boy rocked away.
And they flew through the sky
all Christmas Eve
and didn't come home
until dawn.

For my brother Michael
—*M. P. O.*

To Old Rag Mountain, a source of mystery and inspiration
—*N. B.*

ISBN 0-439-30520-9

Text copyright © 1997 by Mary Pope Osborne.
Illustrations copyright © 1997 by Ned Bittinger.
All rights reserved.
Published by Scholastic Inc.
SCHOLASTIC and associated logos are trademarks and/or registered trademarks of Scholastic Inc.

12 11 10 9 8 7 6 5 4 3 2 1   1 2 3 4 5 6 7/0

Printed in the U.S.A.   08

First Scholastic Trade paperback printing, November 2001

The text type was set in Adobe Garamond.
The display type was hand lettered by Anton Kimball.
Ned Bittinger's paintings were rendered in oil on linen.
Book design by Kristina Albertson